MEM

Tough Boris

Illustrated by

KATHRYN BROWN

PUFFIN BOOKS

With special thanks to Allyn Johnston, Janet Green,

Joe, Paul, BZ, and Eric

— K.B.

PUFFIN BOOKS

Published by the Penguin Group
Penguin Group (Australia)
250 Camberwell Road, Camberwell, Victoria 3124, Australia
(a division of Pearson Australia Group Pty Ltd)
Penguin Group (USA) Inc.
375 Hudson Street, New York, New York 10014, USA
Penguin Group (Canada)
90 Eglinton Avenue East, Suite 700, Toronto, Canada ON M4P 2Y3
(a division of Pearson Penguin Canada Inc.)
Penguin Books Ltd
80 Strand, London WC2R 0RL England
Penguin Ireland
25 St Stephen's Green, Dublin 2, Ireland
(a division of Penguin Books Ltd)
Penguin Books India Pty Ltd
11 Community Centre, Panchsheel Park, New Delhi – 110 017, India
Penguin Group (NZ)
67 Apollo Drive, Rosedale, North Shore 0632, New Zealand
(a division of Pearson New Zealand Ltd)
Penguin Books (South Africa) (Pty) Ltd
24 Sturdee Avenue, Rosebank, Johannesburg 2196, South Africa

Penguin Books Ltd, Registered Offices: 80 Strand, London, WC2R 0RL, England

First published by Harcourt Brace & Company
6277 Sea Harbor Drive, Orlando, Florida 32887-6777, USA
This edition published by Penguin Books Australia, 2010

23 22

Text copyright © 1994, Mem Fox
Illustrations copyright ©1994, Kathryn Brown

The moral right of the author and illustrator has been asserted.

Printed and bound in China by South China Printing Co. Ltd.

National Library of Australia
Cataloguing-in-Publication data:

Fox, Mem, 1946– ..
Tough Boris.

ISBN 978 0 14 056453 2.

I. Brown, Kathryn, 1955– . II. Title.

A823.3

The illustrations in this book were done in watercolours on Waterford paper.
Designed by Camilla Filancia.

puffin.com.au

For Alexia and Helen
and, of course,
Paul von der Borch
– M. F.

For Parker, Sawyer, Will,
Levi, and Amos
– K. B.

Once upon a time, there lived a
pirate named Boris von der Borch.

He was tough.

All pirates are tough.

He was massive.
All pirates are massive.

He was scruffy.

All pirates are scruffy.

He was greedy.

All pirates are greedy.

He was fearless.

All pirates
are fearless.

He was scary.

All pirates are scary.

But when his parrot died,

he cried and cried.

All pirates cry.

And so do I.